Where Thương Keeps Love

By Thu Buu

Illustrated by Bao Luu

WEST
MARGIN
PRESS

This book is dedicated to my wonderful family: Mom, Dad, and all of my siblings, for your constant support and the countless ways you show your love for me. And to my daughter, Nini, for bringing so many dimensions of love and joy into my life. —TB

To my family, thank you for your love and support. —BL

Text © 2021 by Thu Buu

Illustrations © 2021 by Bao Luu

Edited by Clarissa Wong

Library of Congress Cataloging-in-Publication Data
Names: Buu, Thu, author. | Luu, Bao, illustrator.
Title: Where Thương keeps love / by Thu Buu;
     illustrated by Bao Luu.
Description: [Berkeley]: West Margin Press, [2021]
     | Audience: Ages 4-8. | Audience: Grades K-1. |
     Summary: "Inspired by the different ways American
     and Vietnamese cultures think of love, this book
     follows a young Vietnamese American girl who asks
     her friends at school where they store love for their
     parents. She learns that love can be held throughout
     the whole body and that there is not just one
     expression of love" —Provided by publisher.
Identifiers: LCCN 2021013937 (print) | LCCN
     2021013938 (ebook) | ISBN 9781513289434
     (hardback) | ISBN 9781513289441 (ebook)
Subjects: CYAC: Love—Fiction. | Parent and child—
     Fiction. | Vietnamese Americans—Fiction.
Classification: LCC PZ7.1.B896 Wh 2021 (print) | LCC
     PZ7.1.B896 (ebook) | DDC [E]—dc23
LC record available at https://lccn.loc.gov/2021013937
LC ebook record available at
     https://lccn.loc.gov/2021013938

Printed in China

24 23 22 21 1 2 3 4 5

Published by West Margin Press®

WEST
MARGIN
PRESS

WestMarginPress.com

Proudly distributed by Ingram Publisher Services

WEST MARGIN PRESS
Publishing Director: Jennifer Newens
Marketing Manager: Alice Wertheimer
Project Specialist: Micaela Clark
Editor: Olivia Ngai
Design & Production: Rachel Lopez Metzger

Thương has something very special, and she's been looking for the perfect place to keep it safe. "I'll ask my friends at school," Thương thought to herself. She swung her backpack over one shoulder, threaded both arms through the straps, and stepped out the front door.

Walking across the blacktop, Thương spotted her friend Ney headed in the same direction toward their classroom.

Skipping up to him, Thương asked, "Ney, where do you keep love for your parents?"

Ney closed his eyes and thought for a moment. He answered, "I keep it in my head."

"In your head?" repeated Thương with curiosity.

Ney nodded confidently. "Uh-huh. When I try my best, even when something's hard, I learn new things, and that makes my parents happy."

"Mine too!" Thương said.

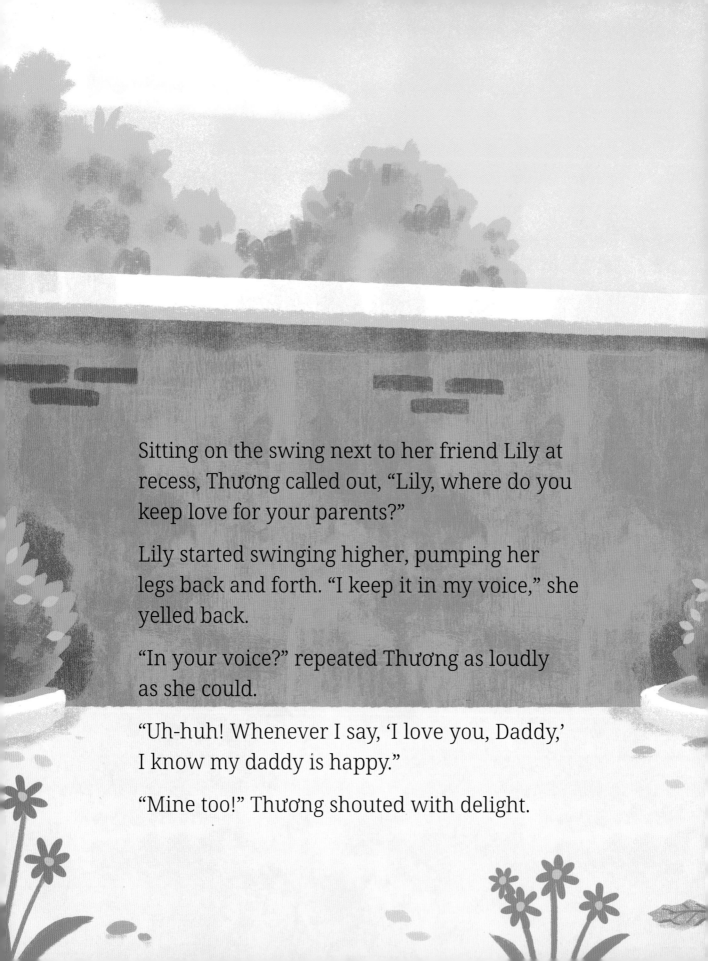

Sitting on the swing next to her friend Lily at recess, Thương called out, "Lily, where do you keep love for your parents?"

Lily started swinging higher, pumping her legs back and forth. "I keep it in my voice," she yelled back.

"In your voice?" repeated Thương as loudly as she could.

"Uh-huh! Whenever I say, 'I love you, Daddy,' I know my daddy is happy."

"Mine too!" Thương shouted with delight.

When Thương and Lily arrived at the lunch table, Carlos was using the end of his burrito to count the golden mini samosas Ney had in his container.

Usually Thương would bring last night's delicious leftovers, like fried rice, stir-fry noodles, or sweet rice and chicken, but not today. Today the cafeteria served corn dogs and chocolate milk. Thương loved corn dogs, especially with ketchup.

Thương took a big bite and swallowed. She then asked, "Carlos, where do you keep love for your parents?"

Carlos wiped his mouth with the back of his hand and sang, "I keep it in my tummy."

"In your tummy?" repeated Thương with a chuckle. An image of Carlos and his family swimming in a pool of chocolate milk popped into her head.

Carlos rubbed his tummy and explained, "When I eat all the veggies on my dinner plate without complaining, my mom is happy."

"Mine too," said Thương. "But I eat my dinner in a bowl," she added.

The last bell rang. School was over. Walking out of the classroom beside Joneisha, Thương asked, "Joneisha, where do you keep love for your parents?"

Joneisha looked quietly at the ground for a moment and then answered, "I keep it in my heart."

"In your heart?" repeated Thương softly.

Joneisha clasped both hands over her heart. "Yes. Every time we do fun things together, my heart is so happy."

"Me too!" said Thương, remembering the fun her family had walking around the neighborhood just the night before.

Stepping through the front gates of the school, Thương spotted Ba waving at her. She broke into a wide grin and skipped toward him.

This was her favorite time of day, when she and her dad walk home together hand in hand. As usual, Thương began telling Ba about her day.

Thương noticed how her dad slightly leaned his ear toward her, listening to every word.

"Oh I see! Ba keeps his love for me in his ears!" she thought to herself.

Their walk home seemed especially short today. She had only just begun describing the yellow dandelions they picked at recess when Ba pulled the latch to open the door to their backyard.

"Hi, Thương," greeted Mệ, waving her hand.

"Did anything new happen at school, con?" asked Ôn as he gestured her over.

"Hi, Ôn Mệ!" Thương replied. She hopped over to the vegetable garden and gave her grandparents each a hug as she retold the dandelion story.

Ôn stooped down and gathered a bunch of freshly pulled carrots with bits of dirt still hanging off their root hairs, while Mệ filled the holes that were left behind.

"Mạ's cooking your favorite tonight—chicken and vegetable stew. These carrots will help make it even sweeter and tastier!" Mệ said.

Thương felt her heart leap with joy.

"Ôn Mệ keep their love for me in the palms of their hands every time they tend our vegetable garden!" she thought.

Around dinnertime, a delicious smell wafted into the living room. Thương followed her nose into the kitchen where she found her mom stirring a pot of stew. Mạ gently lifted her face above the pot and drew in a deep, slow breath.

"Mmmm. I think this needs just a little more salt, and then it'll be perfect. Exactly how you like it, Thương," Mạ said with a smile.

Thương smelled her mom's love rise with each tendril of steam. She smiled back, her heart full of happiness.

"Mạ keeps her love for me in her nose, when she cooks our dinner each night!" she thought.

Thương thought about where her friends keep love for their families, and where her family keeps love for her.

A smile spread across her face.

Before Thương went to bed, she walked up to her parents and expressed her love the best way she knew how—through a game she used to play with her parents when she was learning to speak her first words.

Thương reached up, tapped her head, then bent down and tapped her toes, saying, "Ba ơi, Mạ ơi. Con thương Ba Mạ để từ trên đầu xuống đến dưới chân."

"Daddy, Mommy, I love you, and I keep my love for you on the top of my head all the way down to the tips of my toes."

Thương's parents smiled.

Holding her tightly, together they said, "Ba Mạ cũng thương con để từ trên đầu xuống đến dưới chân."

"We also love you, honey, and we keep our love for you on the top of our heads all the way down to the tips of our toes."

That night Thương went to bed very happy. She had found the perfect place to keep her very special something safe and sound, always and forever.

Expressions of Love

This book was inspired by my perception of the unique differences in the notion of love between American and Vietnamese cultures. When my daughter was born, I enjoyed reading to her. But try as I did, I wasn't able to find a book that expressed exactly how I felt about love.

In American culture, love is often conveyed as an emotion, an affection that is mainly felt. This means people would express and confirm their love by telling one another, "I love you," accompanied by a physical demonstration such as a hug or kiss. In contrast, love in Vietnamese culture seems more tangible, more physical. Perhaps this is why Vietnamese parents rarely verbalize their love for their children. Instead, it's woven into every handsewn pillowcase and served with every steaming bowl of rice. And this may be why Vietnamese children often are just as nonverbal about their love for their parents. Love is expressed in so many ways, and for many Vietnamese, love is often unspoken acts that bring happiness to others.

Say It Like a Vietnamese from Huế

Ba (*Bah*): dad

Con (*Gong*): affectionate term used by an elder to someone younger; also a respectful term used to indicate oneself when addressing an elder

Mạ (*Mah*): mom, term commonly used in the central region of Việt Nam

Mệ (*Meyh*): grandmother, term commonly used in the central region of Việt Nam

Ôn (*Ohng*): grandfather, term commonly used in the central region of Việt Nam

Ôn Mệ (*Ohng Meyh*): grandparents

Thương (*Tuhng*): love

Sing Your Love

Before this book was published, I had created my own hand-bound book to share with my students. Every year for our Mother's Day Tea Party, I would read this story to my class and ask the students to think about where they keep love for their moms, grandmothers, and other female role models in their lives.

I also taught my students a song to sing to their guests. I had learned the song on the next page when I was a little girl, and it helped me celebrate my love for my parents where my voice, muted on matters of love, usually failed me. To me, it shows that love can be expressed through so many different ways, none more correct than the other.

I took liberty with the English translation to maintain the rhyme. However, the essence of the song remains intact.

Yêu Mến Mẹ Cha

Yêu mến mẹ cha yêu trên đầu tôi,
Yêu mến mẹ cha trong quả tim này,
Yêu mến mẹ cha trên hai đầu gối,
Yêu mến mẹ cha yêu toàn thân tôi.

Yêu mến mẹ cha yêu trên bờ môi,
Yêu mến mẹ cha yêu cả lông mày
Yêu mến mẹ cha trên hai gò má,
Yêu mến mẹ cha yêu tràn hai vai.

"I Love My Mom"

I love my mom upon my head,
I love my mom in this heart of mine,
I love my mom upon both knees,
I love my mom with every part of me.

I love my mom upon my lips,
I love my mom with my fingertips,
I love my mom with both my ears,
I love my mom all through the years.

Note: "Mom" can be replaced
by "dad" or a parent's name
at any point in the song.